Copyright © 2012 by NordSüd Verlag AG, CH-8005 Zürich, Switzerland.
First published in Switzerland under the title *Die drei kleinen Schweinchen*.
English translation copyright © 2012 by North-South Books Inc., New York 10017.

All rights reserved.
No part of this book may be reproduced or utilized in any form or by any means,
electronic or mechanical, including photo-copying, recording, or any information
storage and retrieval system, without permission in writing from the publisher.

First published in the United States, Great Britain, Canada, Australia, and New Zealand in 2012
by North-South Books, Inc., an imprint of NordSüd Verlag AG, CH-8005 Zürich, Switzerland.

Designed by Christy Hale.
Distributed in the United States by North-South Books Inc., New York 10017.
Library of Congress Cataloging-in-Publication Data is available.
ISBN: 978-0-7358-4058-4 (trade edition)
1 3 5 7 9 • 10 8 6 4 2
Printed in Germany by Grafisches Centrum Cuno GmbH & Co. KG, 39240 Calbe, November 2011.
www.northsouth.com

The
Three Little Pigs
by BERNADETTE WATTS

NorthSouth
New York / London

There was once a mother pig who had three little pigs.
She was a poor widow and at last had to say to her sons,
"You must go into the world and seek your fortunes."

The first little pig went away and soon met a man with
a bundle of straw.

The little pig said, "Oh please, kind man, give me some
straw so I can build myself a house."

The kindhearted man gave the whole bundle to the pig.

Very quickly the little pig built himself a cozy house and settled in. But after a while a wolf came by and knocked at the door.

"Little pig, little pig, let me come in," called the wolf, licking his lips.

"Oh no! By the hair on my chinny-chin-chin, I will not let you in!" replied the pig, who was feeling tired and was taking a rest.

"Then I will huff and I will puff and I will blow your house in!" said the wolf gruffly.

And the wolf huffed and puffed, and he blew the house in.

In all the confusion, the little pig escaped and ran away.

Then the second little pig left home. As he trotted along, he soon met a man carrying a bundle of sticks.

The little pig said, "Dear man, please give me some sticks so I can build myself a house."

The kindhearted man gave the whole bundle of sticks to the pig.

The little pig built his house of twigs very quickly and moved in.
But soon the wolf came along and tapped on the door.

"Little pig, little pig," called the wolf. "Let me come in!"

"Oh no! By the hair on my chinny-chin-chin, I will not let you in!"
replied the pig, who was rather busy.

"Then I will huff and I will puff and I will blow your house in!" growled the wolf.

And the wolf huffed and puffed, and he blew the house in.

Luckily, the house had two doors, and the little pig escaped through the back door and ran away.

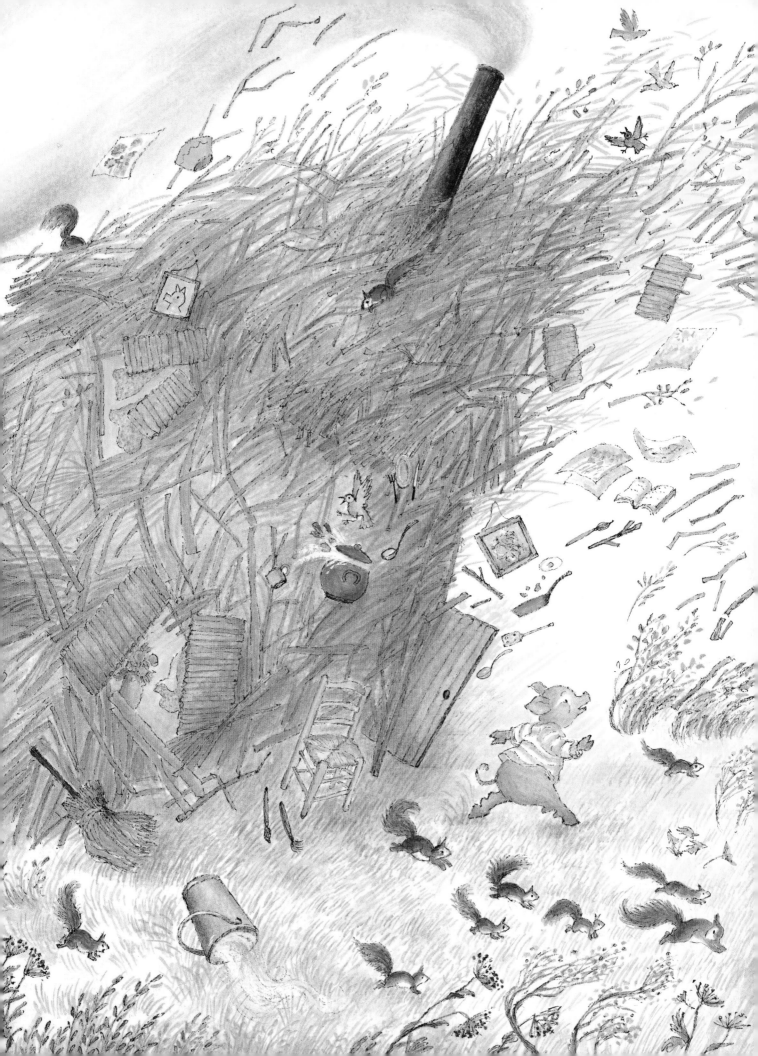

Then it was time for the third little pig to
leave home. His mother was sad to see him go.
Soon the little pig met a man with a load of bricks.

"Oh please, kind man," said the little pig, "let me have some
bricks to build myself a house."
The kindhearted man gave all the bricks to the pig.

Slowly and carefully the little pig built himself a house made of bricks. Then he moved in and settled down. But soon the wolf came by.

The wolf, who was very hungry, knocked loudly on the door and shouted, "Little pig, little pig, let me come in!"

"Oh no! By the hair on my chinny-chin-chin, I will not let you in!" replied the pig.

"Then I will huff and I will puff and I will blow your house in," growled the wolf.

The wolf huffed and puffed, but he could not blow the
house in. Then he rested awhile and thought things over.

"Little pig, little pig, will you just let my paw in?"

"No," said the pig.

"Little pig, little pig, will you just let the tip of my tail in?"

"No!" said the pig very loudly.

"Then I will climb on the roof and come down the chimney."

And the wolf sat outside all night.

Next day, at sunrise, the wolf climbed onto the roof.

But the little pig stoked the fire and got it very hot.

Smoke poured up the chimney, and the wolf got it all in his eyes.

He ran back to the forest, and nobody ever saw him again.

Then the little pig went and fetched his two brothers and their mother, and they still live happily in the little brick house.